Sammy Claws

The Christmas Cat

First published 2018 by Nosy Crow Ltd
The Crow's Nest, 14 Baden Place, Crosby Row, London SE1 1YW
www.nosycrow.com

ISBN 978 1 78800 272 1 (HB)
ISBN 978 1 78800 273 8 (PB)

Text © Lucy Rowland 2018 • Illustrations © Paula Bowles 2018

A CIP catalogue record for this book is
available from the British Library.

Papers used by Nosy Crow are
made from wood grown
in sustainable forests.

Printed in China
10 9 8 7 6 5 4 3 2 1 (HB)
10 9 8 7 6 5 4 3 2 (PB)

For Billy and Charlotte xx
L. R.

For Mr and Mrs Claus x
P. B.

Sammy Claws
The Christmas Cat

Lucy Rowland
and
Paula Bowles

nosy crow

Sleepy old Sammy Claws, Santa's pet cat,
was furry and purr-y and fluffy and fat.
He liked nothing better than having a snooze
in a box . . . or a cupboard . . . or snuggled in shoes.

And as Sammy dozed
he would dream of the day
that he'd travel with Santa
up high in his sleigh.

"Tomorrow is Christmas Eve!" Sammy Claws said.
He yawned a big yawn then he curled up in bed.
"I'll help in the morning, then Santa Claus might
just take me along on his sleigh for the night!"

But . . .

23 December

. . . when Sammy woke again,
hours had passed!

"Am I too late to help?"

he cried, dashing off fast.

He ran to the workshop and leapt past the elves.
The door swung behind him...

ELF & SAFETY

and **toppled** the shelves!
The presents went flying —
oops! —
past Santa's head.

"Oh, Sammy,
we're busy!
WATCH OUT!"
Santa said.

Poor Sammy crept off and he looked rather sad.
"I wanted to help," he thought. "Now I feel bad.
I'm sure Santa won't let me fly with him now.
There must be a way to say sorry, but how?

RIBBON-O-MATIC

Perhaps while I think I'll just rest for a minute."
He found a big box . . . and he slowly climbed in it.

The elves worked so hard. There was so much to do!
But sleepy old Sammy Claws hadn't a clue.
Sammy just wanted to doze for a while...

but his box was wrapped up
and then placed on a pile.

OUT

IN

Magic Dust

At six o'clock Santa was ready to go.
He jumped in the sleigh with a loud, "Ho! Ho! Ho!"
He held the reins tightly, got ready to fly . . .

and off they all sped through the starry night sky.

Now, during the trip, they were going so fast
that Sammy woke up from his snooze at long last.
But what a surprise for poor Sammy the cat.
He found he was stuck in a box!
Fancy that!

He scrabbled around then he gave a loud shout . . .
but nobody heard . . . and he couldn't get out!

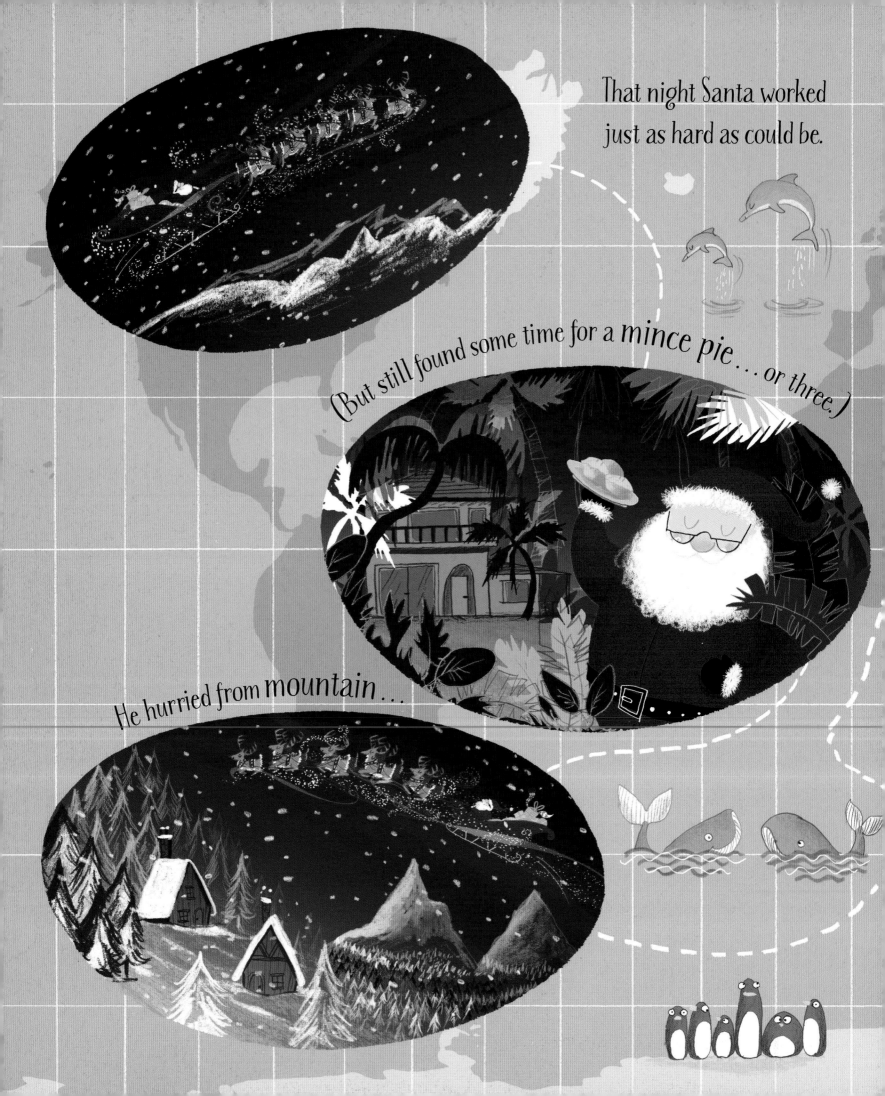

That night Santa worked
just as hard as could be.

(But still found some time for a mince pie . . . or three.)

He hurried from mountain . . .

to seaside . . .

to town.

He found all the chimneys . . .
and quickly climbed down.

But in such a rush, with the lamplight so dim . . .
he didn't see two **robbers** waiting for him.
Their names were Bad Billy and Mischievous May.
They wanted to **steal** all the presents away!

They climbed on the sleigh
and they crouched really low
as Santa set off with his sack
through the snow.
"We'll grab 'em," said Billy,
"as soon as we can!"

But Sammy Claws heard every word of the plan.
"A plot to rob Santa? We'll see about that!
I'll soon stop those villains!" thought Sammy the cat.

Now, at a big castle (somewhere south of France),
as Santa set off, May hissed, "Quick! Here's our chance!
Just look at those presents! That's such a big pile.
Delivering those will take Santa a while!"

"Let's **snatch** all these presents!"
said Bill with a scowl.

They reached for a box,

but …

...it let out a YOOOWWWLLL!
Then out sprang a shape and it flew through the snow
all covered in paper, some string and a bow.

They fell in a snowdrift, head first, and — what luck! —
those mischievous robbers were both firmly stuck.
Police cars arrived on the scene with a wail
as Sammy looked on with a flick of his tail.

When Santa popped out of the chimney, "Ho! Ho . . .
Oh!" what was that down on the ground far below?
Two robbers? Police cars? And what a surprise . . .

"It's Sammy the cat!" Santa rubbed at his eyes.
"However did Sammy get all the way here?"
But as Santa puzzled it soon became clear.

"You were wrapped in a present,
but then you broke free
and frightened those robbers away!
Now I see!"

He hugged Sammy tight
as they climbed in the sleigh.
"Oh, Sammy," said Santa,
"you've saved Christmas Day!

From now on," he promised,
"we'll work as a team!"
And Sammy Claws grinned
like a cat with the cream.

What **fun** they both had
as they worked through the night.
And as they flew home
Sammy closed his eyes tight.

He thought to himself,
"Oh, next year will be great!
Unless I'm too sleepy ...

No! What if I'm late?"

But Santa had saved one last present, you see.
A brightly wrapped parcel sat under the tree.
And Santa was smiling.
They heard a tick -tock . . .

What was
Sammy's
present . . . ?